D0949978

Praise for
JAMES PATTERSON

"All Patterson's success stems from one simple root: his love of telling stories."
—**Washington Post**

"James Patterson's books for young people are wildly popular for a reason—the author has an almost uncanny knack for understanding exactly what his readers want and serving it up in a way that feels fresh and new every time. Daft jokes, familiar settings, and memorable characters…but Patterson is not in the business of serving up literary junk food—his stories always bring real substance to the table."
—**Teachwire**

"Anyone who can get some of us kids to say, 'Please give me another book' is quite an amazing author."
—**Kidsday, Newsday**

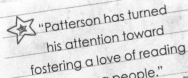
"Patterson has turned his attention toward fostering a love of reading in young people."
—**Los Angeles Times**

Praise for BECOMING MUHAMMAD ALI

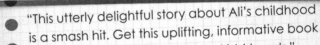

"Cassius Clay's kinetic boyhood—depicted through prose, poetry, and illustration—is the prism through which this uplifting novel casts the myth of the legendary boxer."
—**New York Times, Best Children's Books of the Year**

"This utterly delightful story about Ali's childhood is a smash hit. Get this uplifting, informative book onto library shelves and into kids' hands."
—**School Library Journal, starred review**

"Patterson and Alexander, two heavyweights in the world of books, unite to tell the story of how Cassius Clay grew up to be Muhammad Ali, one of the greatest boxers of all time."
—**The Horn Book, starred review**

"The prose and poems reflect Clay's public bravado and private humbleness as well as his appreciation and respect for family and friends. A knockout!"
—**Booklist, starred review**

"Spare...witty...Cassius's narrative illustrates his charisma [and] drive...Powerful, accessible view of a fascinating figure."
—**Publishers Weekly, starred review**

"A stellar collaboration that introduces an important and intriguing individual to today's readers."
—**Kirkus Reviews, starred review**

"These lightning-bolt figures are poetry surrounded by prose...a kinetic, dazzling experience...Like the world many adolescents inhabit, the world that Becoming Muhammad Ali presents is complex...But most importantly, it's a reminder that once upon a time Cassius Clay, all poetry and italics, was a kid like the rest of us. It is my hope that Black children read this book, see themselves in young Clay and know that they too are poetry made flesh."
—**New York Times Book Review**

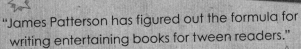

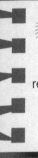

A **MIDDLE SCHOOL** STORY

DOG DIARIES

DINOSAUR DISASTER

Jacky Ha-Ha: A Graphic Novel
Jacky Ha-Ha: My Life Is a Joke (A Graphic Novel)

KATT VS. DOGG
Katt vs. Dogg
Katt Loves Dogg

MAX EINSTEIN
Max Einstein: The Genius Experiment
Max Einstein: Rebels with a Cause
Max Einstein Saves the Future
World Champions! A Max Einstein Adventure

MIDDLE SCHOOL
Middle School: The Worst Years of My Life
Middle School: Get Me Out of Here!
Middle School: Big Fat Liar
Middle School: How I Survived Bullies, Broccoli, and Snake Hill
Middle School: Ultimate Showdown
Middle School: Save Rafe!
Middle School: Just My Rotten Luck
Middle School: Dog's Best Friend
Middle School: Escape to Australia
Middle School: From Hero to Zero
Middle School: Born to Rock
Middle School: Master of Disaster
Middle School: Field Trip Fiasco
Middle School: It's a Zoo in Here

TREASURE HUNTERS
Treasure Hunters
Treasure Hunters: Danger Down the Nile
Treasure Hunters: Secret of the Forbidden City
Treasure Hunters: Peril at the Top of the World
Treasure Hunters: Quest for the City of Gold
Treasure Hunters: All-American Adventure
Treasure Hunters: The Plunder Down Under

Becoming Muhammad Ali (cowritten with Kwame Alexander)

Best Nerds Forever

Laugh Out Loud

Not So Normal Norbert

Pottymouth and Stoopid

Public School Superhero

Scaredy Cat

Unbelievably Boring Bart

Word of Mouse

For exclusives, trailers, and other information, visit jimmypatterson.org.

A **MIDDLE SCHOOL** STORY

DOG DIARIES

DINOSAUR DISASTER

JAMES PATTERSON

WITH STEVEN BUTLER
ILLUSTRATED BY RICHARD WATSON

JIMMY Patterson Books

Little, Brown and Company

New York   Boston

Copyright © 2021 by James Patterson

Illustrations by Richard Watson

Cover art by Ellie O'Shea. Cover design by Tracy Shaw.
Cover copyright © 2022 by Hachette Book Group, Inc.

JIMMY Patterson Books / Little, Brown and Company
Hachette Book Group
1290 Avenue of the Americas, New York, NY 10104
Kids.JamesPatterson.com

Originally published in Great Britain in 2021 by
Penguin Random House UK

First US Edition: April 2022

JIMMY Patterson Books is an imprint of Little, Brown and Company, a division of Hachette Book Group, Inc. The Little, Brown name and logo are trademarks of Hachette Book Group, Inc. The JIMMY Patterson Books® name and logo are trademarks of JBP Business, LLC.

The publisher is not responsible for websites (or their content) that are not owned by the publisher.

Library of Congress Cataloging-in-Publication Data
Names: Patterson, James, 1947- author. | Butler, Steven, author. | Watson, Richard, 1980- illustrator. Title: Dinosaur disaster / James Patterson ; with Steven Butler ; illustrated by Richard Watson.
Description: New York : Little, Brown and Company, 2022. | Series: Dog diaries | "A middle school story" | Audience: Ages 7-12 | Summary: Junior leads his pack of dog friends on a sneaky mission into a museum to steal dinosaur bones for Lola's midnight birthday feast.
Identifiers: LCCN 2021039589 | ISBN 9780316334631 |
ISBN 9780316334730 (ebook)
Subjects: CYAC: Dogs—Fiction. | Diaries—Fiction. | LCGFT: Animal fiction. | Humorous fiction.
Classification: LCC PZ7.P27653 Di 2022 | DDC [Fic]—dc23
LC record available at https://lccn.loc.gov/2021039589

ISBNs: 978-0-316-33463-1 (paper over board),
978-0-316-33473-0 (ebook)

Printed in the United States of America

LSC-C

Printing 1, 2022

To Teddy and Ralphy
—S.B.

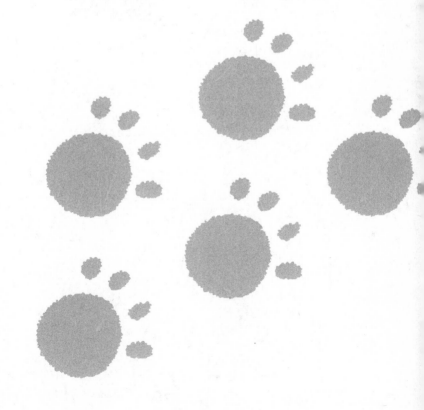

Junior
Catch-A-Doggy-Bone

OH BOY! OH BOY! OH BOY!

You've picked up this book in your five-fingery-digits at just the right moment, my person-pal. You must have been practicing really hard to improve your sniff-a-licious senses and your houndy honing skills, huh!?!

If you've nosed your way through my DOG DIARIES in the past, HELLO AGAIN! It's BRILLIANT to see you're back for more fun!

And if you haven't, my name's JUNIOR. JUNIOR CATCH-A-DOGGY-BONE! But we don't have time for proper introductions and courteous butt-sniffs right now...Oh, don't worry your human-heart...there'll be plenty of time for all that snuggly cuddle-umpcious stuff in a little while, but first, I have to tell you about the latest news, my furless friend! It's something so EXCITING...so unbelievably BARKTASTIC...my tail has been wagging for days. IT WON'T STOP!

Okay...okay...if I'm going to do this and let you know how TERRIFIC my news is, I need to set the scene properly.

First things first. Close your eyes.
Oh no, wait...scratch that...if you close

your person-peepers you won't be able to read my MUTT-MANUAL. Maybe just squint your eyes a little? Yeah, that ought to do it…

Now, this may sound a little crazy, but I want you to play make-believe with me. It'll be worth it; I cross my houndy-heart!

Let's cast our minds back into the far distant reaches of the past, my person-pal…just imagine it!

No, further than that!

FURTHER STILL!
KEEP GOING!

WE'RE HEADING

THE

PREHISTORIC

THE DAWN

I think we've arrived, my person-pal. We have successfully cast our imaginations all the way back to the very beginning of Hills Village.

Picture this…

We're in a dark, overgrown forest filled with amazing things to sniff and taste and chew. Everywhere we look there are GIGAN-TIC prehistoric sticks that make us drool like a Shih Tzu at snack time. Stickiest-sticks like those would take the likes of you and me a whole week to gnaw through, so we can't get distracted now.

There are strange and spine-jangling noises all around us and the only light is coming from a gap in the bushes up ahead. Let's sneak over a take a peek…

Now, brace yourself, my furless friend. We're about to peer through the gap in the undergrowth and what you're going to see will have you pooping your person-pants with shock and surprise if you're not prepared.

Are you ready?

Okay, cue the big dramatic music. You know, the type with lots of drums…SUPER BOOMY ONES…

DUM-DA-DA-DUM-DUM-DA-DUUMMM!!!!

Here goes…

AGGGGGHHHHH! Have you ever seen anything so MUTT-NIFICENT in your life?! We've arrived in the JAW-RASSIC period!

And we're in luck, my person-pal. If you want to see more, all you have to do is use your imaginary binoculars. Let's take a closer look at the beasts of our epic expedition. And don't worry, they don't call me "GENIUS JUNIOR: THE EXPLORER-DOG EXTRAOR-DINAIRE" for nothing, you know?

Well...umm...nobody actually calls me that...but I'm an expert on all these weird and wild dino-roars, I swear!

C'mon, I'll teach you everything ~~I've just made up~~ I know...

Behold! The toothy TERRIER-SAURUS REX. It's the fiercest predator of chew toys in the valley and is the nastiest nipper too.

Here, you can see the long-necked BRONTO-PAW-RUS. Able to snaffle snacks from even

TERRIER-SAURUS REX

the highest shelves in their pet human's cave-kennels.

BRONTO-PAW-RUS

Over by that volcano, you can see the TREAT-CERATOPS. The vacuum cleaner of the Jaw-rassic plains! It can sniff out even the tiniest crumbs of ancient Doggo-Drops or Crunchy-Lumps in the long grass, leaving nothing for the other dino-roars to enjoy.

TREAT - CERATOPS

The skies overhead are filled with loop-the-looping TONGUE-Y-DACTYLS, the lickers of the prehistoric world. No cave-human's face is safe from a ferocious, waggy-winged licking when these overexcited critters swoop down.

TONGUE-Y-DACTYL

Then…over by the Triassic Trash Cans you can see my favorite of them all. THE RACCOON-O-DON! I tell ya, my person-pal, I could bark my barkiest bark at these sneaky little dino-dumpster-divers until my snout turns blue and my whiskers explode into flames! They're just so…

HUH?!?! What's that?

THE RACCOON-O-DON!

Suddenly, just as we're enjoying the AMAZING view and thinking about chasing a few raccoon-o-dons, the music gets louder and more drum-tastic and then...DUM-DA-DA-DUMMM...the ground beneath us begins to quake.

Before we know it, the dino-roars scamper in every direction, thundering all around us back to their cave-kennels, as lava explodes from the distant mountains! It's time to get out of here, my furless friend!

AGH! It looks like I may have got a little over-excited on my DINO-DAYDREAM! We'll be squished under a dino-paw in seconds if we're not sizzled into bow-wow buns first!

Quick, Junior! Think us both back to our own time again! Hurry, hurry!

Don't worry, my person-pal, I can do this. I can fast-forward us to the HILLS VILLAGE of today, filled with tummy rubs, Triple-Cheesy-Nacho-Nosher burgers, and hugs with my best-best-BESTEST pet human, Ruff!

KA-BOOM! We made it! Run and hide someplace safe...anywhere! In the laundry pile! In the Rainy Poop Room and lock the door! Under the bed where you keep your secret stash of midnight snacks!

Phew! Thrilling as that was, my person-pal, I certainly am glad to be back in the warm confines of my sniff-a-licious home. Safe from snarling teeth and deadly dino-claws...

HA HA! What am I saying? I know we were only playing make-believe, really, but there's a super IM-PAW-TANT reason I wanted to show you all those magnificent mutt-monsters from yester-yap. I'll explain it all to you, I promise, but just before I do, I simply have to let out a few BARKY-BARKS. I've held it together since you opened this book, but I just can't resist any longer. It feels so good to know you're reading it, my furless friend!

As I was saying earlier, when you picked up my FABULOUS mutt-manual, if you've read any of my Dog Diaries before you'll know all about the WONDERFUL human family I live with in our cozy kennel. But, if you haven't, there's no time like the present to introduce you to my person-pack.

Here they are!!!

Just look at their happy smiling faces… well…all except Jawjaw…but she's not the person I want you to meet the most.

~~THE KHATCHADORIAN FAMILY~~
THE CATCH-A-DOGGY-BONE PACK

~~MOM~~
Mom-Lady

~~GEORGIA~~
Jawjaw

~~GRANDMA~~
Grandmoo

~~RAFE~~ Ruff

I can't wait to introduce my very own pet human! My bedtime buddy! My scratchy, tummy-tickling cuddle companion. The BEST KID in the whole of Hills Village...no, the WORLD...no, THE UNIVERSE!

RUFF!

Even the sound of his name makes my tail go crazy! I mean it, my furless friend! At 4 p.m. when Ruff gets home from school every day, I can't help planting a zillion licks on his FANTASTIC face (Ha ha! Maybe one of my far-off ancestors was a tongue-y-dactyl?) and performing the Happy Dance!

Okay, Junior, calm down! Breathe in... breathe out...breathe in...breathe out.

So, there we have it, my furless friend. Now you've met Ruff and the Catch-A-Doggy-Bone pack, none of us are strangers and I think you're ready for me to explain just why I took you on an imaginary journey back to the Jaw-rassic period to investigate the dino-roars of old...

You see...well...umm...I saw one!

Just a few days ago, right here in Hills Village!

Now, wait a second. I know what you're thinking. You're getting ready to throw this book out the window, screaming...

ARTIST'S IMPRESSION

And you'd probably be right if it weren't for one thing...I really did see a dino-roar thundering along the street, and...SO DID RUFF AND A WHOLE BUNCH OF MY BUDDIES AT THE DOG PARK! I wasn't the only one, so I can't be making it up, right?

I bet you're at least a little intrigued now, aren't you?

I KNEW YOU WOULD BE!

Would you like me to tell you what happened? Ha ha! What a stupid question...of course, you would!

Well, it all started last Sunday...

Last Sunday

10:51 a.m.

Sigh. It was a good day, my person-pal. It's the middle of summer and Ruff is home from school all the time! Can you imagine how WONDERFUL that is?

I'd already had a yum-a-lumptious breakfast of my favorite dogfood, Meaty-Giblet-Jumble-Chum, while Ruff, Mom-Lady, and

Jawjaw had their wifflies with moo-poo syrup. Ha! Human food is so weird!

Anyway, we'd enjoyed a deliciously lazy morning. I had already snuffled around the backyard and had my usual poop and pee. I'd done some very important barking at joggers out on the front sidewalk, and then I walked Ruff to the Dandy-Dog store to pick up some extra weekend treats and a new chew toy (I had been a particularly GOOD BOY that week. Agh! I love those two words!).

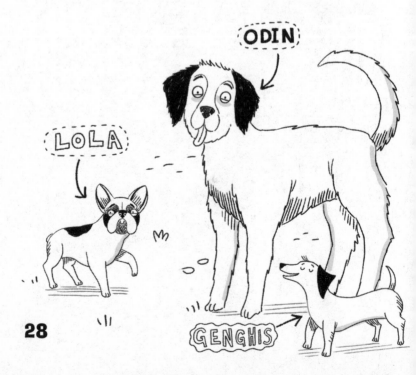

Now we were in the dog park along with my best pooch-pals on the planet.

I tell ya, my furless friend…I love that pack of mangy mutts from the tip of my snout to the end of my twitchy tail. Each and every one of 'em!

We've been through a WHOLE LOT OF CRAZY CHAOS together since we all escaped from pooch prison at HILLS VILLAGE DOG

SHELTER and found happy human families to live with...We've dealt with CANINE CRIMINALS, dastardly DOG SHOWS, stolen TREASURED TOYS, the HOWLY WIENER, a man named SAINT LICK who visits your kennel during a human holiday called CRISP-MOUTH, speeding hot tubs hurtling down-hill, VEGETARIAN vacations, MONSTERS terrier-izing the neighborhood...and that's only a fraction of the weird stuff that's happened to us lately!

So, you can imagine we were pretty certain there were no more surprises coming our way. How could anything beat the weird-ness we'd already seen?

That morning, as Ruff was chatting to the other pet humans and we were sunning our-selves snoozily near the jungle gym, we felt sure that absolutely nothing bonkers was

coming our way. Lola's birthday was coming up on Thursday and we were happily making plans for the big day...

I was so excited, my person-pal. I'd been secretly planning WAY in advance and had already found Lola the most AMAZING birth-day gift EVER!

I mean it! This one was a real winner. Even better than the muddy stick I found for her last year, and that's saying something!

You see, occasionally...DON'T TELL MOM-LADY...I sneak out through the loose board in the backyard fence and have a little snoop around town all by myself.

What?! Even the goodest of the GOOD BOYS has to have some time to himself every now and again. Feel the wind beneath his paws and...umm...is that what you furless folk say? You know what I mean...Anyway, on my last solo expedition around Hills Village, I was minding my own business and decided to go for a snuffle through the junkyard.

It's a favorite spot of mine. Somewhere I can unwind and explore a few new smells, or maybe chew on the arms of an abandoned comfy squishy thing...whatever takes my fancy.

So, I had just turned the corner by the mountain of rusty tin cans, when I spotted it!

The best-BEST-BESTEST birthday present for Lola!

It was sitting there on an old truck tire, going crusty in the sunshine, and I knew she'd LOVE it! It was a dog's dream!

There isn't a mutt in the whole world who doesn't love the exotic aroma of a lost sock. It tastes and smells of all the delicious places it has been and is just as fascinating to us as

a good book is to you human-types.

SSSSSHHHH! Don't tell anyone, but I've had it stashed under Ruff's bed ever since I found it. I can't wait to give it to my stinky little friend on her special day!

But…I know what you'll be thinking now, my furless friend. You're still wondering about that dino-roar I mentioned, aren't you? You're scratching your human-head trying to figure out why I'm talking about making plans for Lola's party when I've teased you with the arrival of a prehistoric pooch-a-saurus in Hills Village.

Well, hold on to your haunches, because this is the point where our peaceful day suddenly gets very exciting…

10:58 a.m.

We were still all yapping and yowling over what would be the best way to celebrate our friend's special day when the little birthday-pooch sat up from her snoozing and grunted.

Do you smell something? Something d...d... DELICIOUS!

She turned to us looking more snout-sniffingly serious than I'd ever seen Lola look before.

All of us stuck our noses in the air and sniffed the breeze curiously.

At first I only caught the whiff of the snack cart selling human food and the tingly scent of a kid eating potato chips on a bench, but then...once my dog senses had sifted through all the sniff-a-licious nearby smells... oh MY!

I swear to you, my person-pal, it was like nothing I'd ever smelled in my entire life... and I've sniffed and snuffled A LOT of interesting and scrum-a-lumptious things in the past.

Our pet humans didn't notice, of course, but in a few moments, every dog from the jungle gym to the duck pond had their snout in the air and was savoring the unfamiliar aroma drifting our way.

IT WAS INCREDIBLE!

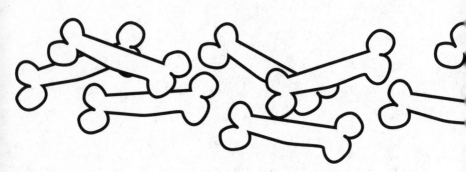

41

I'm amazed we didn't wash ourselves clean out of the park with the all the drooling going on. The smell was completely WON-DERFUL and it was getting stronger!

Whatever was giving off this INCREDIBLE perfume was getting closer and, as it did, my

nose was picking up more and more auda-cious little aromas. There was smoke, and salt, and cut grass, and poop, and dry leaves, aaaaaannnndddd…

Lola yelped so loudly I thought her lit-tle round head was about to rocket off her shoulders!

Before anyone had time to growl or bark a warning, an ENORMOUS creature raced into view from behind the trees at the edge of the park.

Its LOOOOONNNNNGGGGG neck arched up high into the air and at the end of it, a bul-bous skull glowered scarily.

While the rest of my pooch-pals frantically scampered to the safety of the trash cans, I was rooted to the spot in fear and awe. I rec-ognized the beast the second I saw it.

Don't forget I know ALL about this stuff, my person-pal. I've spent hours and hours on the comfy squishy thing with Ruff watching moving pictures, and there was no mistaking it...

This monster looming into view was a dino-roar! A BRONTO-PAW-RUS, if I've got my dino-roars right. But it was...well... it was...a lot skinnier than I imaged it would be. Maybe it was sick? Or hungry? Or both?

Huh...on the picture box, the bronto-paw-ruses in the moving pictures looked a lot more scaly and gray-greenish. This one seemed way more gristly and bony...and flat.

FLAT!!!

That's when I realized it wasn't something to be scared of, my furless friend. How could I have been so stupid? The bronto-paw-rus racing around the edge of the dog park

44

was painted on the side of GIANT moving people-box…What's the Peoplish word for it? Oh yeah…A TRUCK! It wasn't a real dino-roar, but the delicious smell coming from it certainly was real.

My paws sprang into action and, before I even knew what I was doing, I was sprinting toward the truck as it continued on its journey along the edge of the bushes.

I reached the gates at the entrance of the park, stumbled out onto the sidewalk, and…

I knew it. I just knew I recognized that smell. It wasn't the scent of BRONTO-

PAW-RUS. It wasn't a living, breathing creature...It was a great big pile of delicious, crunchy, chew-a-riffic, mouthwatering, belly-bungling BONES!!!

My houndy-head was suddenly swirling with a squillion questions, my furless friend, and I simply had to find out more about this strange feast inside the truck. Why was it here? Where was it going? WHAT DOES IT TASTE LIKE?!

I could hear Ruff yelling and shouting as he ran to catch up with me. Any minute now he'd come dashing through the park gates and clip the leash to my collar, and that would be the end of it. My adventure would be over before it started!

Now, I'm not proud to tell you this, my person-pal, and I knew I was risking being called the worst two words in the whole universe…BAD BO…BAD B…AGH! I don't think I can even bring myself to say it…but I'd never smelled anything so completely BARKTASTIC in my life, and I just had to find out more. Plus, my poor pooch-pack had all dived behind the trash cans and would never know what they were missing if I didn't do a spot of investigation on their behalf. It's only polite, y'know.

So…I RAN!

11:07 a.m.

The truck chugged and screeched its way across Hills Village, with me galloping along behind. I followed it around past the grocery store and up the hill to where all the big whiffly kennels are on the far side of town.

For a second, I thought it was going to keep on going and head straight off into the sunset, until it turned with a squeal of brakes onto a road I'd never ventured along before.

Ruff and Mom-Lady don't head this way when we're out on our morning walks together, and I could feel the fur on the back of my neck bristling with excitement. There, standing at the end of the short boulevard, was the biggest building I'd EVER seen! It was huge! Twice as big as the Hills Village town hall and FIVE TIMES bigger than the Dandy-Dog store.

A crowd of humans had already gathered outside it and they all started to clap and cheer as the truck approached.

What in the world was going on?

Doing my best to look as innocent as possible, I carefully snuck into the group of people, weaving in and out of their hopping and shuffling feet, until I managed to peek out through the front of the gathering.

I swear, I'd never been more exhilarated in my life, my furless friend. The truck had stopped in front of a strange new building that looked scary and fun all at the same time. There were huge windows and pillars, and the smells wafting from the open front doors were even more tantalizing and tummy-twisting than the truck full of bones that had just thundered through town.

I was about to sneak a little closer when my own paw touched something crinkled and rustly on the sidewalk. It was a flyer of some sort and I stared down at it, trying to use my slightly crummy understanding of the Peoplish language to read what was written on it.

I recognized the word for "dino-roar" straight away, but the big letters at the top of the flyer were much trickier.

I tried it out in my head...
MMM-UUU-SEE-UM
No, that wasn't quite right.
MMM! YOU-SEE-MMM
Nearly, but not perfect.
MMM! YOU SEE 'EM?
Yes! That's it! It was a question! The flyer was making yummy sounds and then asking if I'd seen the delicious pile of treats being delivered.

What could this incredible building be?

Whatever it was, the exotic whiffs drifting out through the front door told me it was filled with mouthwatering snacks.

With my tongue hanging out and my jaws drooling, I took another step closer to the **MMM! YOU SEE 'EM?** and...

Ruff grabbed me from behind, clipped the leash to my collar, and yanked me away.

Except for the night of Howly Wiener... and Iona Stricker's obedience classes... and the attack of the TERROR-TURKEY at Fangs Giving...Oh, and being made to eat vegetables at a houndy health retreat... being dragged away by my angry pet human while the truck drove under an archway and disappeared around the back of the MMM! YOU SEE 'EM? might have been one of the most distressing moments of my life.

Ruff was hopping mad! I can't say I blame him...I know I would have been fuming if he'd run off across town without me, but there was no way I could have done things any differently.

As we walked home to the Catch-A-Doggy-Bone kennel in perfect silence, my mind was racing. How could I call myself the INTERNATIONAL MUTT OF MYSTERY if I didn't find a way to get back to the giant building and get a peek at the BRONTO-PAW-RUS bones again?

I'd be the laughingstock of Hills Village if everyone knew I got so close to tasting that HUMONGOUS chew toy and then got yanked away by my pet.

One thing was for sure...I was going to have be SUPER sneaky.

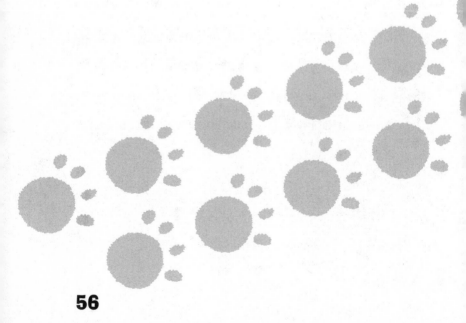

Wednesday

10:17 a.m.

So, here we are, my person-pal. You've caught up with all the craziness that happened last Sunday.

It's been three days since I saw the BRONTO-PAW-RUS bones and it's all I've been able to think about. I see it in my dreams! I smell it in the laundry pile! I can taste it in my water bowl!!!

58

I can sense the cogs turning in your person-brain as you're reading this, my furless friend. "DID YOU MAKE IT BACK TO THE MMM! YOU SEE 'EM?" I hear you ask.

Well, the answer to your question is very simple...NO!

Ruff was so upset that I ran away from him across busy streets, he told Mom-Lady and Jawjaw when we got home and now, I'm in a great big heap of trouble.

It seems that when I wrecked the Catch-A-Doggy-Bone kennel to save the family from Saint Lick...or when I stole Iona Stricker's hot tub and used it as a slippery getaway vehicle for my old friend Mama Mange...or just when I helpfully howl for hours to let the mailman know I'm ready to eat today's mail... Mom-Lady has mistaken all those things for naughtiness!

61

I didn't even have time to run and hide under the bed before she pointed her finger in my face and yelled…

Can you imagine the horror, my person-pal? I haven't been out on the leash for a trot about town, or to see my pooch-pack for THREE WHOLE DAYS!!! This is torture! I've had nothing to do except peeing and pooping in the backyard and sniffing around the hallway closet to make sure my archnemesis, the vacuum cleaner, is behaving itself.

At mealtimes, I've been presented with a bowlful of kibble! Just dry, BORING kibble! No Meaty-Giblet-Jumble-Chum! No Crunchy-Lumps or Doggo-Drops!

AND...Mom-Lady insisted that Ruff gave me a bath after we arrived home!

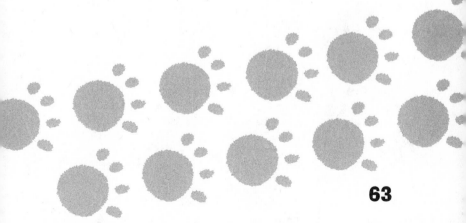

It's been pretty miserable, my furless friend. No dog should be cooped up in their kennel like a big old cluck-hen when they've been such a GOOD BOY!

To make matters worse, that night the whole of the town was clamoring with dogs barking in their backyards about the delicious-smelling monster that reared its ugly head near the Hills Village dog park. From what I could hear, most of the neighborhood pooches were pretty scared and worried, especially after the case of the MYSTERY MUTT who terrier-ized the locals, stealing treats and toys alike.

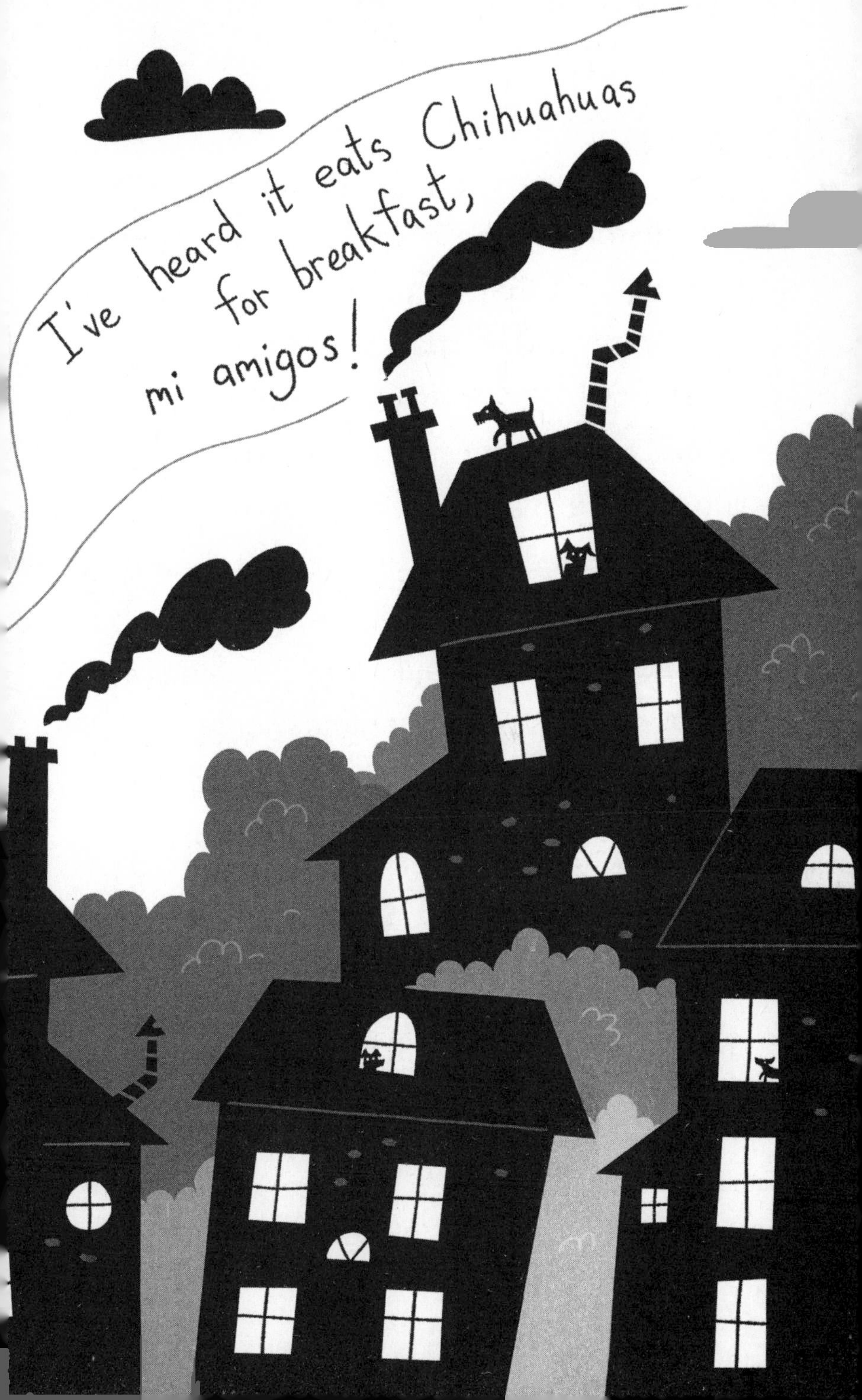
I've heard it eats Chihuahuas for breakfast, mi amigos!

I can't place my paw on why, but something stopped me from putting everyone's mind at rest that evening. I didn't even tell my dearest pooch-pack! With a few informative howls I could have let everyone know there was no monster and it just a picture on the side of a truck with a big pile of DELICIOUS bones inside, but I didn't. I guess I was a little scared that if I told everyone, the whole feast would be crunched and slobbered-down by the time Mom-Lady let me out of punishment-prison.

10:39 a.m.

BORED! Ruff has gone off to the shops with Mom-Lady and I'm stuck indoors with Jaw-jaw. She's such a sour-faced complainypants and has NEVER liked me. How could any-one not like ME?! I took her my favorite ball, I chewed one of her shoes with love, and I even did a Happy Dance for her, using my best puppy-dog eyes! Nothing moves that girl!

10:59 a.m.

This is THE WORST! I dozed in a patch of sunlight on the Food Room floor and was dreaming about the BRONTO-PAW-RUS in no time at all.

Huh...that was a weird one, but it's made me hungry just the same. If I don't get out of here soon, I'm going to die from dino-deprivation!

11:01 a.m.

If there's one thing I know that Jawjaw can't stand, it's whining...which is funny because she does so much of it herself. HA HA!

All I need is a few well-placed scratches and whimpers at the backyard door and she's sure to let me out, even though Mom-Lady told her not to until she got back from the grocery store.

Here goes...

Hmmm...I may need to ramp this up a gear or two...

Worry not, my person-pal...I've only just begun to exercise my howly talents. Watch this!

Ha ha! What did I tell you, my furless friend? You didn't think I'd be stuck indoors for ever, did you?

Now that I've made it as far as the backyard, all I have to do is wait until Jawjaw has gone back to her room and can't see me, and...

oooooo!!!

GO! GO! GOOOOO!

11:04 a.m.

Quick! Follow me, my person-pal. We just need to wriggle under the loose board in the fence to FREEDOM!

11:05 a.m.

If I keep my snout to the ground, I can get all the way to the MMM! YOU SEE 'EM?, have a good snuffle about to check out what WON-DROUS treats they're keeping inside, and be back home before Mom-Lady and Ruff have even finished shopping.

11:17 a.m.

Check! Check! This is Special Agent Junior Catch-A-Doggy-Bone ready for action!

Here we go, my person-pal. I've reached the MMM! YOU SEE 'EM? and I sure am ready to SEE 'EM!

Last time I was here, just before Ruff grabbed me and dragged me away, I saw the truck driving though an archway and vanishing around the back of the building. If I follow where it went, I just know my super-sensitive nose will pick up that delicious whiff and lead me to the BRONTO-PAW-RUS bones.

The MMM! YOU SEE 'EM? looks different from how it looked on Sunday, my furless friend. There are HUGE banners hanging outside with pictures of dino-roars on them…

If that banner is telling the truth, there could be more than one pile of dino-bones just waiting to be savored by a pooch like me. I'm going to take a closer look, my fur-less friend. The coast is clear...

11:20 a.m.

I can barely stop myself from drooling all over my front paws!

I followed the scent of the BRONTO-PAW-RUS bones around the back of the great big building, my person-pal, and was hit by the most enormous gust of dusty, moldy, oldy, dirt-lectable smells.

It seems to be coming from a great big door in the back wall of the MMM! YOU SEE 'EM?...

11:22 a.m.

AGGGGGGGHHHHHHHHHH!!!!! I…I…I DON'T KNOW…I'VE FORGOTTEN HOW TO SPEAK, MY FURLESS FRIEND. THERE… THERE ARE…SO…SO…SO MANY…I FEEL DIZZY…MIGHT FAINT…

Get a grip, Junior!

Just give me a moment…

Just one more moment…

One more…

Okay…I'm okay…You'd better make sure you're ready for what I'm about to show you, my furless friend. I have some pants-pooping news for you and you're going to squeal like a Dalmatian with a new pack of Doggo-Drops when you see it.

Are you ready? GOOD!

I just crept up to the big doors, peeked inside through the crack, and saw THIS!!!

Never in my wildest dreams could I have imagined there would be a treasure-trove like this in Hills Village! I can't believe the humans have gathered together such a feast for us pooches. They're SO kind sometimes!

It just has to be a special surprise for us...I'm sure of it! AGH! WHAT AM I SAYING?! IT MUST BE FOR LOLA'S BIRTHDAY!!!

Lola's pet human MUST have arranged this whole thing for his pooch and her mutt-mates. That's got to be what it's for. Why else would anyone collect so many TERRIFIC-smelling bones to be gnawed on???

People don't even eat bones, right?! It's something I've wondered at all my life. Why on earth do you human-types not enjoy gnawing on a juicy bone that's been buried in the dirt for safekeeping? It's brain-boggling!

But enough of that for now…something's happening…

Through the crack in the door I can see two humans walking this way. They must be the official feast organizers. They're probably coming to congratulate me for being the first dog in Hills Village to discover the surprise!

11:27 a.m.

WHA?!?! I…I…I don't understand, my furless friend. When I saw the two humans coming to greet me, I sat there in front of the big double doors in my best GOOD BOY pose.

What human (besides Jawjaw) could resist it?

Well, it turns out, these two brutes could!

The door swung open and they marched out with angry faces.

No dogs allowed? What was that lady talking about? How are we supposed to have a giant feast for Lola's birthday if we can't go inside? It's madness! It's stupid! It's...

I just thought of something, my person-pal. What if...what if this isn't a feast for dogs at all? What if it's a feast for humans? Maybe I was wrong about people not eating bones? Maybe my Catch-A-Doggy-Bone pack is just broken? Maybe Ruff, Jawjaw, and Mom-Lady are bonkers non-bone-eaters and I had no idea. AGH! I'll never live it down if after all this time it turns out my pet humans are the only anti-gnawers in the whole town.

It's too heartbreaking to think about. Us poor deserving dogs will have to watch through the crack in the door as hungry humans crunch and munch their way through this prehistoric picnic!

11:56 p.m.

I don't think I've ever felt more miserable in all my life, my furless friend. My jowls are droopy, my tail is tucked under, and my paws are ploddy.

I'm amazed I managed to make it back to the Catch-A-Doggy-Bone kennel before Ruff and Mom-Lady arrived home with the groceries.

When they both walked in, I couldn't even bring myself to perform the Happy Dance.

90

I suppose that's one good thing to come out of this unhappy news. Mom-Lady thought I was a melancholy mutt because I'd been stuck at home for too long and ungrounded me right there and then.

Little does she know…

4:33 p.m.

I'm trying so hard to look on the bright side of things, my person-pal. I really am. I don't want to be a down-in-the-dumps dog for Ruff. Especially after I made him mad by running away.

C'mon, Junior…All I need is to think of a few positive things about not being invited to the big, bony bonanza at the MMM! YOU SEE 'EM?

Right…umm…well…there's…

Ooh, at least I hadn't told Lola about the feast yet. This way she never has to know and won't be disappointed on her birthday.

Then there's…umm…I guess all the humans will be very happy, which is a reason to make me happy, right? Who knows…maybe Ruff will have a go at gnawing on his first juicy rib and learn to love it?

And…and…I won't get extra full-up and explode from all the amazing food I'm going to miss out on. And I suppose it is possible for a dog to be too happy…
Yep! I'm so lucky not to be allowed at the feast I could almost jump for joy…

Who am I kidding?! I can't do it, my person-pal! I can't pretend this is good news.

I need some serious tummy-rubs and cuddles, that's for sure. I'll go find Ruff. He'll be in the Picture Box Room right about now, watching his favorite action adventure series, *Ninja Knockout Nine*...Maybe he can cheer up this mopey mutt.

4:57 p.m.

AAAAAAAAAAAAAGGGGGGHHHHHHH! I was wrong again, my furless friend! Things are so much worse than I imagined!

There we were, Ruff and I, snuggling on the comfy squishy thing watching an episode of *Ninja Knockout Nine*, when a commercial break came on.

Low and behold, right there on the picture box was an ad for the MMM! YOU SEE 'EM? and their room filled with dino-roar bones.

It turns out...it turns out...IT TURNS OUT THE HUMANS AREN'T GOING TO EAT THEM AT ALL!

That was the final straw, my personal-pal. If the human-types were planning to eat the skeletons like they're supposed to, then at least someone would be having a tasty treat-a-licious time.

BUT!!! They're not planning that at all! I just discovered from the picture box that you humans put the dino-bones in a big room and then you...you...LOOK AT THEM! THAT'S IT?! YOU DON'T EVEN GIVE THEM A SNIFF OR A LICK? IT'S A CRIMINAL ACT

OF EXTREME WASTEFULNESS! WHAT'S
WRONG WITH YOU ALL?!

Excuse me while I bury my head in the
laundry pile and cry myself to sleep, my furless friend.

5:26 p.m.

I'm still in the laundry pile,
my person-pal. I have to tell
you, I've been lying here
trying to understand why the
humans of Hills Village would
dig up all those delicious
dino-roar bones and then not
enjoy their gristly goodness,
but I just can't figure it out.

I bet even the dino-roars
themselves would be
confused.

Just look at that!

97

6:00 p.m.

Mom-Lady was feeling a little guilty about keeping me cooped up for so long, I think, and has given me a great big bowl of Meaty-Giblet-Jumble-Chum for dinner.

It's my absolute favorite meal, but for the first time in my licky-life, I...I...I don't know if I can eat it, my furless friend! I'm looking down at the yum-a-lumptious globs of meat and jelly and all I can think about is that poor BRONTO-PAW-RUS. I'm seeing visions of it in my bowl again. I can practically hear it moaning...

99

7:01 p.m.

OH, GIMME A BREAK!!! My people-pack have all settled down in the Picture Box Room for a snuggly evening and Mom-Lady insisted on watching THE NEWS! It's a super BORING show designed to put humans to sleep, in case you don't know.

I was kinda hoping she'd let us watch *Ninja Nannies From Outer Space* or *Mutant Man 7000*...those are some of Ruff's and my favorites...but nope! Mom-Lady insisted.

Anyway, I was drifting off into a dino-daydream while the man on the screen was yammering on, when...

I can't escape it, my furless friend! I'm doomed to be reminded of all the SNACK-A-LICIOUS SNACKS I won't be snacking on for the rest of my snackless life.

100

Sunday is going to be the worst. Mom-Lady told Ruff and Jawjaw she wants to go to the MMM! YOU SEE 'EM? to look at the dino-roars.

LOOK AT THEM?! AAAAGGGHHHH! It's torture!

9:27 p.m.

I can't do it, my person-pal! The story about the dino-roar exhibition played on repeat all evening. It's all anyone could talk about and I...well, I've done a lot of thinking. A LOT!

Now, I know what you're going to say when I tell you that I've come up with a plan and it's not quite what a GOOD BOY would do, but hear me out, okay?

You're about to gasp and point one of your five-fingery-digits, yelling, "JUNIOR! When did

102

you become such a BAD BOY?" but I have to do this…I JUST HAVE TO! I'm going to sneak into the MMM! YOU SEE 'EM? tonight and sample just a few tiny bones. Teensy ones!

Believe me, I can't bear the thought of being called a BAD BOY again by Ruff, but it's now or never! I just can't call myself the INTERNATIONAL MUTT OF MYSTERY if I don't at least try.

AND…it's not entirely selfish…

I've decided to tell all my pooch-pals as well and we can surprise Lola with a birth-day feast of prehistoric proportions! She deserves it, the little cuddle puddle. I can picture her happy grin as she's munching on some monstrous morsels.

Lola is one of my favorite dogs in all the world, and I couldn't live with myself if I didn't do this special treat for her. Suddenly the

AMAZING sock I found for her in the junk-yard just isn't enough and will never do.

So...promise you won't tell anyone?

Ha ha! I knew I could trust you, my fur-less friend. You're shaping up to be a true HOUNDY-HERO and I couldn't be prouder of you.

It's nearly time for me to go out into the backyard for my last pee of the evening. It's at the same time every night. Mom-Lady is nothing if not reliable. Ha ha!

I always go out when the long hand of the time-circle points down to the floor and the short hand points across to the cupboard where the plates are kept. That's 9:30 p.m. to us dogs, but I don't know what you humans call it.

104

Anyway…once I'm outside, I'll put my master plan into action. Here's what I've come up with…

It's foolproof, my furless friend. I'll keep you posted with how it goes, so wish me luck.

AGH! I can hear Mom-Lady coming to let me outside. BE STILL MY HOUNDY-HEART!!!

11:48 p.m.

Shhh! Don't make any loud noises, my person-pal. Ruff and the rest of my Catch-A-Doggy-Bone pack are all finally asleep. It took ages for Jawjaw to get off the phone to her school friends, but even she's dozed off now. I can hear her snoring through the wall… HA HA…and it's time to get out of here.

You'll be pleased to know my plan worked perfectly earlier! I'm a total pro-pooch at cooking up clever schemes after all.

While I was out in the backyard for my last

pee of the evening, I faced the bushes and pretended to be yowling at RACCOONS in case Mom-Lady or Ruff were watching, while secretly calling Odin, Diego, Betty, Genghis, and Lola in our Doglish language that none of my pet humans can understand.

We've agreed to meet outside the MMM! YOU SEE 'EM? at midnight. They're going to be wondering why on earth I've called them all there. I can't wait to surprise them!

YIKES! I haven't got long. I'd better get across town SHARPISH, my person-pal, or I'll be late for my own adventure!

Midnight

Phewy! I don't think I've run that fast since Iona Stricker tried to blame me for her ruined flower beds just before the night of Howly Wiener!

So, here we are, my person-pal. Everything outside the MMM! YOU SEE 'EM? was still and silent, and, for a moment, I thought I might be the only one of my pack who'd made it. Until…

t!
WHA?!
This had better be good, Junior... I was snoozing!
What's that amazing smell in the air?
Is everything all right?

I knew I could count on my AMAZING mutt-mates to show up for a spot of excitement. They NEVER let me down.

I told my pals all about the BRONTO-PAW-RUS skeleton and the grand exhibition in the MMM! YOU SEE 'EM? I described the commercial I'd seen and how it turns out that humans only like to look at dino-delicacies and not taste them...and then I explained all about my plan to sneak in for Lola's midnight birthday feast!

111

12:02 a.m.

I can hardly stop my tail from wagging, my furless friend. With every step we take toward the MMM! YOU SEE 'EM?, the tongue-twitchingly tasty waft of all those ancient bones gets stronger.

Now we just need to get inside...

I may be an INTERNATIONAL MUTT OF MYSTERY, but breaking into a great big building like this is new to me.

I think I've got an idea, though.

When the two security guards...what were their names? I can picture their badges right in front of me...ummm...Albert and Gloria, I think it was. Yep! That's it...When Albert and Gloria came out of the back doors and shooed me away, I remember Albert saying...

I told you I spotted a mutt on the security camera!

Because I'm probably the smartest mutt this side of...ummm...the universe...it just so happens that I know all about security cameras. IT'S TRUE!!! I learned everything there is to know about that stuff from watching *Ninja Knockout Nine* with Ruff. On that show, they're always sneaking into buildings while avoiding the security cameras.

So, if I lurk around the back doors for a while, the security cameras will spot me and Albert and Gloria will come to investigate, just like they did last time. Then, once the doors are open, we just need to figure out a way to get past them...

12:04 a.m.

Here goes, my person-pal. I've told my pooch-pack to hide a little way off while I sit outside the back doors and wait...the guards are bound to recognize me from the other day and come out to see what I'm up to.

12:05 a.m.

Hmmmm...nothing...Maybe a little door-scratching will do the trick?

12:06 a.m.

Where are those two? They must have seen me by now. Are they snoozing?

12:07 a.m.

That does it, my furless friend, for the second time today I'm going to have to unleash the "LET ME OUT!" howl that I used on Jaw-jaw earlier. Only, this time it's a "LET ME IN!" howl. Ha ha!

I'm going to have to think on my paws when they open those doors, my person-pal. My canine cunning won't let me down. I just know it. Wish me luck...

12:13 a.m.

WOO-HOO! We're in, my furless friend!

But it did not go to plan AT ALL...we nearly didn't make it!

Don't panic! I'll explain...

After a few seriously jaw-jabbering howls, I waited for the guards to come to the door. BUT, suddenly I heard a noise behind me... The guards must have come out a different door!

My lick-tastic instincts kicked in and, as Gloria moved to grab me by the collar, I leapt up like a houndy-hero and grabbed

It's that dog again!

the big ring of
keys from her
five-fingery-
digits.

I ran off
with the
MMM! YOU
SEE 'EM?
guards in hot pursuit and called to my
pooch-pack to follow. I had to find the door
the guards had come out from!

It didn't take me long, my person-
pal. I saw the open
entrance and dived
inside. The rest of
my pooch pack
had sprinted past

117

Albert and Gloria and followed just behind me. Before the guards could catch up with us I slammed the door shut, locking Albert and Gloria outside.

PHEW! That was a close one...But now us mutts HAVE THE WHOLE PLACE TO OURSELVES!

I tell ya, my furless friend, my tail has gone into waggy overdrive!

This is going to be the BEST birthday Lola will ever have had and I'm prancing-paw-proud to be the dog who came up with the idea.

I'd say it's time we go have a sniff about... C'mon...

12:24 a.m.

Ooooh, grown-up humans can be a strange bunch, I swear! If you're anything like me, my person-pal, and you've never been to a MMM! YOU SEE 'EM? before, I bet you wouldn't be able to guess the weird things locked away in here.

We snuffled our way through huge halls and long corridors filled with all kinds of strange and interesting things to taste and play with...

121

What can I say, my furless friend? It was pretty easy to get distracted in that place with so many new smells. But we had delicious dino-roar bones to find and no time to waste.

So we crept further and further into the museum, when suddenly...THE DELICIOUS WAFT OF DINO-ROARS caught our attention. We must be getting close to the AMAZING room I'd glimpsed through the back doors of the MMM! YOU SEE 'EM?

We turned the corner and...THERE IT WAS! THE GREAT HALL OF BONES!!!

It's time to get ready for the BEAST OF FEASTS! We're about to have the most SNACK-TASTIC PREHISTORIC PARTY there has ever been!

122

1:31 a.m.

I...I...I don't know what happened, my fur-less friend. You won't believe me when I tell you, but right now I'm back at the Catch-A-Doggy-Bone kennel hiding behind the comfy squishy thing.

I thought I'd be jabbering on to you about our incredible monstrous meal and all the birthday fun we had with Lola, but instead I'm cowering in the shadows of the Picture Box Room feeling more confused than a Rottweiler on a roller coaster.

I'll...I'll try to explain. Bear with me...

Y'see...We all ran excitedly into the Great Hall of Bones and were nearly swept off our paws at the sight of so many tongue-

twitchingly
toothsome
treats.

It's the most beautiful thing I've ever seen...

Lola looked like she was about to burst into tears with happiness.

Everywhere we looked there were towering beasts of bone. We didn't know where to start!

We eventually chose a little TWIG-O-SAURUS for an appetizer, and we were just about to dive in for a good gnaw, when...

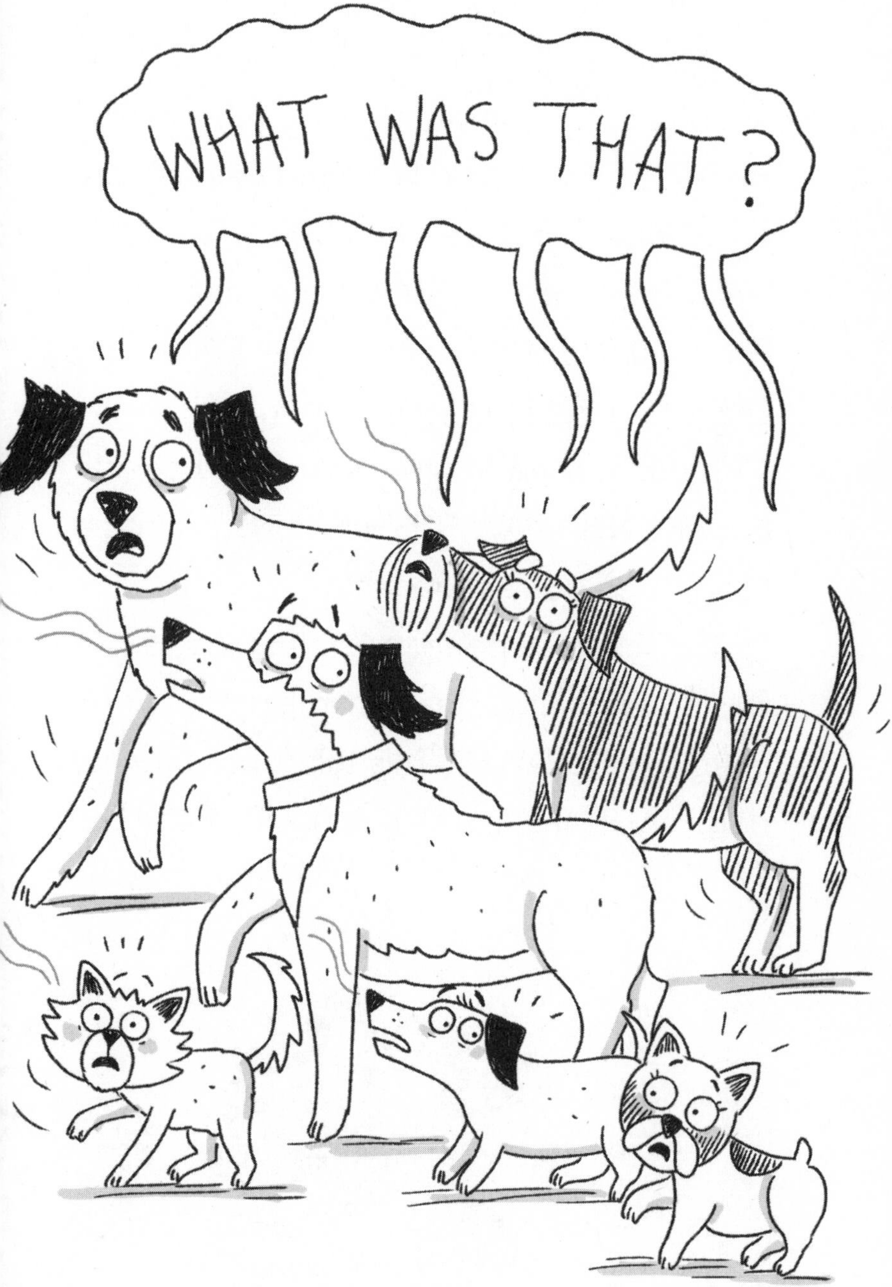
WHAT WAS THAT?

Something triggered our sniff-a-licious senses and we knew we weren't alone. The smell was a mixture of flowery perfume, lemon-scented shampoo, and smugness. For a second, I thought maybe Albert and Gloria had got back inside…but…no…

There lurking in the shadows beneath the BRONTO-PAW-RUS was a…a shape…a thing…a…I don't know what.

The shape stepped toward us, and I saw it was dressed in black and had a dino-roar rib in its paws…PAWS?! This thing was another dog, and it was snacking on OUR FEAST!!!

127

With one more step, the mystery mutt stepped into the open and I saw it was…

I swear, my jaw nearly dropped off and rattled across the floor, my person-pal. Duchess! The pampered poodle princess pet of Iona Stricker,

What are you doing here, you mangy pack of canine criminals?

Don't even think about it! These are mine!

128

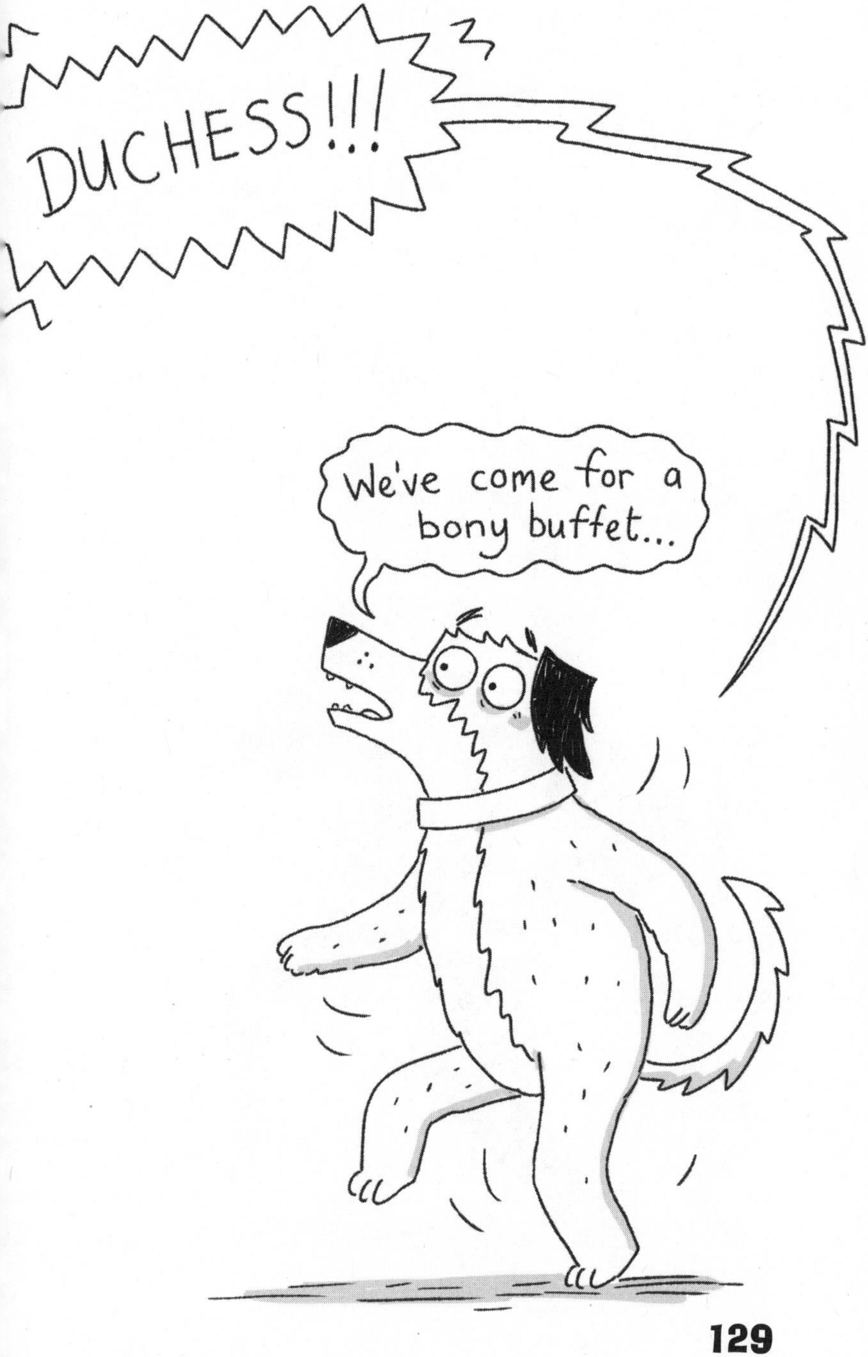
DUCHESS!!!
We've come for a bony buffet...

the meanest old moaner in Hills Village, had broken into the MMM! YOU SEE 'EM? and was snaffling the juiciest bones BEFORE US! How had this happened?!

With that, Duchess bounded to the nearest wall and pressed the alarm button before we could even think about trying to stop her.

Suddenly, there was Cretaceous chaos everywhere. Alarms sounded, lights flashed, shutters started lowering across all the doorways! It was madness, my person-pal. I watched in BARK-WILDERMENT as Duchess leapt into an open ventilation grate in the wall, taking the BRONTO-PAW-RUS bone with her.

The police will be on their way! You'll all be back in pooch prison by morning... HA HA!

POOCH PRISON!!!

There was no way we were going to stick around and allow that to happen, my furless friend.

We all managed to scamper out of the Great Hall of Bones just before the gates closed, then we tore through the corridors in a complete pooch-panic. My nose was still filled with the delicious whiff of DINO-ROAR and I couldn't find the scent to show us which way we'd come.

I tried to spot things I recognized...

Weird bandage lady? CHECK!
Rusty metal guy? CHECK!
Angry security guards? CHECK!

AGH! ANGRY SECURITY GUARDS?! As if we didn't have enough to worry about, Albert and Gloria had managed to get back inside the building and were sprinting toward us.

134

135

All I can say is thank goodness for shiny floors and furry bellies, my person-pal. Otherwise I think we'd all be back in the Hills Village Dog Shelter by now.

And that was that, my furless friend. We managed to dart out through the open doors and hide in the bushes just before the policemen and policewomen showed up with sirens blaring.

We searched for Duchess once all the fuss had died down, but she was long gone.

Sigh...we didn't even get a teensy taste before that pompous poodle ruined our plans. It's official, my person-pal...I am one miserable mutt.

Duchess may have won this round, but there's no way I'm giving up on Lola's birth-day feast. I just need to figure out a way to get back into the MMM! YOU SEE 'EM? for a second attempt before Duchess does.

But, right now, I guess I'd better sneak

back to bed in Ruff's Sleep Room before he notices I'm gone.

See you in the morning, my furless friend.

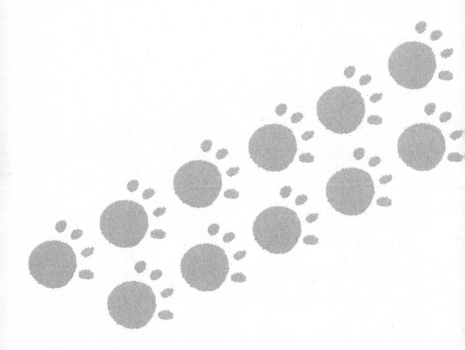

Thursday

10:57 a m.

Ooh, my barky-blood could boil, my per-son-pal. Ruff and I have just left the dog park and you can guess who I saw there, parading about like a pampered princess. Yep. Duchess!

I was over by the jungle gym with my pooch-pack when Iona Stricker came walking across the playing field with her slippery sidekick trotting along behind.

I could hear the haughty human boasting about how delightful her dog was...HA! She has no idea her precious Duchess is a canine criminal!

Duchess pretended she hadn't spotted me until Stricker turned her back, and then the horrible hound gave me the snobbiest, snootiest sneer I've ever seen!

It was a look that said, "DON'T EVEN THINK ABOUT RETURNING TO THE MMM! YOU SEE 'EM? TONIGHT!"

140

Well, I've got news for that primped perpe-trator...my amazing pooch-pack is ready and raring to go. We'll stop Duchess from stealing our dino-roar dinner if it's the last thing we do!

THE FEAST FIGHT IS ON!!

2:37 p.m.

Come on!!! Come on!!!! I swear to you, my furless friend, I might be great at lots of things, but I'm terrible at being patient. I've been staring at the time-circle on the Food Room wall for the past hour.

I can't wait to get back to the MMM! YOU SEE 'EM? tonight to protect our bony-bounty from Duchess's drooling jaws.

I guess all this waiting is a good time to make a plan...

142

OPERATION FLY-AWAY FLUFFY!

1. Snaffle crumbs from under the Food Room table.

2. Scatter crumbs outside the

MMM! YOU SEE 'EM?

3. Attract hundreds of birds.

4. Tie birds' feet with laces from all the shoes in the hallway closet.

5. Tie the other ends to Duchess.

6. Is it a rocket? Is it a plane? No, it's a pampered pooch! HA HA!

Maybe?

Agh! Maybe not. There aren't enough laces in the Catch-A-Doggy-Bone closet for that many birds...

I'll have to think on my paws when the time comes, my person-pal. Iona Stricker's dastardly dog is as slippery as hot dogs fresh from the trash! But we'll be ready for her...

10:32 p.m.

Not long now, my person-pal. I've been whiling away the hours counting dino-roars in my head, but it looks like Ruff, Jawjaw, and Mom-Lady are finally getting ready to head to their beds.

I can practically taste our victory over

Stricker's pompous poodle, and the WON-DERFUL feast that's going to follow it.

I'll keep you posted...

11:09 p.m.

It's time, my furless friend! My humans eventually dozed off after what seemed like an eternity and I snuck out the back door and through the loose board in the fence, alerting my pooch-pack on the way.

I got to the MMM! YOU SEE 'EM? a few minutes ago and there's no sign of Duchess, which means I'm here before her. Perfect!

Oh, and here comes my pooch-pack now...

11:12 p.m.

Albert and Gloria, the security guards, are outside patrolling the building. Maybe they're not so stupid after all. So we're hiding in the bushes until the coast is clear... Shhh! Don't make a sound, my person pal. We could be here for a while.

11:27 p.m.

We're in! The guards finally moved out of sight, moaning and muttering, giving us enough time to figure out how to use the keys I swiped from Gloria last night.

It took Odin ages to find the right one and get it turned in the lock, but eventually we made it fit and opened the door.

Then, it was just a case of retracing our steps, through the rooms and corridors until we found it again...THE GREAT HALL OF BONES!

It smells even better than it did yesterday and we're all desperate to chow down on some Triassic treats...but first we have to wait for Duchess to arrive so we can trap that cunning canine...

11:31 p.m.

Still no sign of Princess Prim...Where is she?

11:45 p.m.

Still nothing...

11:51 p.m.

Maybe the pampered poodle finally admitted to herself that there's no way she could outsmart Junior and his AMAZING pooch-pals and has given up? Ha! I bet that's it... she's probably back in her kennel sulking as we speak.

11:57 p.m.

I spoke too soon, my furless friend. Just as we were starting to think Duchess definitely wasn't coming, we heard a creak coming from the ventilation grate.

11:58 p.m.

Hold your breath, my person-pal. DON'T MOVE A MUSCLE! Duchess has just jumped down to the polished wooden floor and she's here in the GREAT HALL OF BONES with us! It's now or never if we're going to stop this canine criminal. This is waggy-tailed warfare!

I need to think of something quick...
ummm...think!

I...well...errr...oh no! If Duchess takes two
steps closer, she'll sniff out our hiding place
and she'll have the upper hand...THE UPPER
PAW!

12:14 a.m.

HA HA! Well, okay...I may not have been too
fast-thinking back there, but...ummm...it's
not my fault. Y'see, I...I was overexcited and
I hadn't eaten my usual pre-bedtime snack of
Crunchy-Lumps followed by a Denta-Toothy
chew.

Anyway, before I had time to concoct the
perfect plan and Duchess even knew what
hit her, my BRILLIANT pooch-pals, Odin and
Diego, came to the rescue.

In all my fussing about the paw-fect plan, I hadn't even noticed those two sneaking over to the wall by the TREAT-CERATOPS and…

It was TERRIFIC, my furless friend! The drenched dog landed right in the middle of the grand entrance hall like a flailing, flopping poodle-puddle!

Of course, it alerted Albert and Gloria, but I don't even mind! We managed to escape back the way we'd come, and we watched

Does she belong to you, ma'am?

from the bushes with glee as Iona Stricker showed up to collect her misbehaving mutt. The guards must have found her number on Duchess's collar. HA HA!

That was probably the best thing I have ever seen in my life! So, we didn't get to have Lola's birthday feast on her actual birthday, but we'll come back tomorrow, and this time there'll be no Duchess to spoil our fun. There's no way Stricker will be letting her prize poodle out of the house for about a gazillion years!

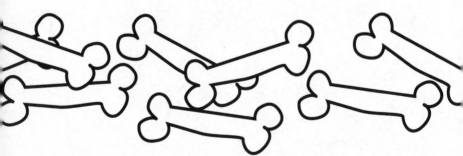

Friday

Junior's Friday Plans

8:00 a.m.: Breakfast

8:30 a.m.: Second breakfast

8:45 a.m.: Possible third breakfast?

9:00 a.m.: Think about how dino-roar bones taste

10:00 a.m.: Think about Duchess getting caught and laugh

11:00 a.m.: Think about dino-roar bones and Duchess getting caught

11:45 a.m.: Poop

12:00 p.m.: Lunch!

1:00 p.m.: Snooze in the sunshine

3:00 p.m.: Wake up laughing, remembering how Duchess got caught

4:00 p.m.: Walkies in the dog park, meeting my pooch-pack to plan tonight's feast

5:00 p.m.: Pre-dinner snack

6:00 p.m.: Dinner!

7:00 p.m.: Snuggle up with Ruff on the comfy squishy thing, watching the picture box

9:00 p.m.: Start thinking about which dino-roar I'm going to nibble on first

10:00 p.m.: Wait impatiently for my person-pack to go to their Sleep Rooms

11:00 p.m.: When everyone is asleep, sneak out SUPER quietl

158

11:30 p.m.

Check! Check! Special Agent Junior and his secret pooch-pack are back again, my furless friend, and this time, we're not leaving without our monstrous meal!

I swear I've been yipping and yapping with laughter all day about last night's craziness. I bet Ruff thinks I've gone bonkers...Ha ha! It was just so FANTASTIC knowing that Duchess didn't get away with her traitorous trouble for once. It'll teach her for trying to ruin our feast, the mutt-meanie.

If the humans in your neighborhood are anything like the ones in Hills Village, they will love a good gossip, and Duchess was all everybody was talking about at the dog park today...HA HA! Iona Stricker didn't show her face, but she's going to be hopping mad when she finds out her obedient-babykins is the talk of the town!

So, we're back again at the MMM! YOU SEE 'EM?, my person-pal, and Duchess won't be able to sneak out tonight after getting caught. Stricker will probably have locked up their kennel tighter than POOCH PRISON! We'll be free to snaffle and snack our way through the GREAT HALL OF BONES without any horrible hounds to bother us...so long as we can stay out of Albert and Gloria's way, but that shouldn't be too tricky.

THIS IS IT! We're finally going to feast! Brace yourself for the most SNACK-TASTIC night of your life, my furless friend!

160

11:.57 p.m.

AAAAAAAAAGGGGHHHH!!!

I can't believe it, my person pal! THOSE STINKERS HAVE CHANGED THE LOCKS!!!

Our one way of getting into the MMM! YOU SEE 'EM? has been taken away from us!

We tried all the keys in all the doors, but NONE OF THEM WORK!

Not only that, the place is CRAWLING with guards. Hundreds of them! Albert and Gloria must have called their guardy-guy-and-gal-pals for backup. We were only outside for a few minutes before we heard humans running our way and had to scamper into the bushes.

WHAT ARE WE GOING TO DO NOW?!?!

Saturday

10:27 a.m.

Last night was just the worst, my person-pal. I could hardly sleep…I just couldn't stop thinking about being denied our delicious dino-feast.

This morning I was so exhausted and stressed that I only ate ONE breakfast!

Ruff and I are just getting ready to go to

the dog park. I'll have to find the energy to try to lift the spirits of my mutt-mates. Especially Lola...she must be so disappointed to not get her birthday bonanza.

Maybe I'll take her the old sock I found in the junkyard. It might make up for not filling our bellies with delicious dino-treats...It might...

11:53 a.m.

HOLD EVERYTHING!

I have big news, my person-pal!

I was at the dog park earlier, trying to cheer up my pooch pals...not even the stinky old sock could raise a happy yip...when I found this stuck on a twig next to the gates where we pee.

I'd know that prissy paw print anywhere. It's Duchess…

What is that devious dog up to?

11:57 p.m.

I thought about it all day, my furless friend, and I'm here at the dog park. I know you're probably thinking that I'm being a foolhardy-hound and this is just another trap set by my archest of feasty enemies...but desperate times call for desperate measures, my per-son-pal. I'd never forgive myself if I don't try everything to get Lola her belated birthday feast.

Plus...my pooch-pack is hiding out in the long grass and will spring out to rescue me if anything goes head-over-tail.

11:58 p.m.

Waiting...waiting...waiting...

11:59 p.m.

Starting to get nervous, my person-pal... What if we're hanging around the jungle gym while Duchess is snaffling our prehistoric pic-nic? What if she's laughing at us? What if...

Midnight

Just as my paws were getting sweaty and my tummy was groaning with nerves, my BRIL-LIANT ears heard a faint rustling from the flower beds near the restrooms.

You guessed it...Duchess has arrived.

WORK TOGETHER?!?! With that prim pampered poodle?!?! There's no way! I wouldn't dream of it! I could never stoop so low! I'd be the laughingstock of Hills Village! I'd be letting down my pooch-pack! I'd be…

Oh, no! She's ri…she's righ…I can barely bring myself to admit it, my furless friend, but Stricker's precious pet is…is…RIGHT!

12:10 a.m.

You should have seen the looks on my pooch-pals' faces when I told them the new plan.

So... we're going to share the feast...
Are you feeling okay?
No, mi amigo!
I guess there's lots to go round...
Duchess is allowed a tiny crumb...that's all.
Can we just get to the feasting part?

12:27 a.m.

I swear, I never dreamed this would ever happen, my person-pal, but even I have to admit that Duchess is a master of sneakiness. If we're going to get past the HUNDREDS of guards now patrolling the MMM! YOU SEE 'EM?, we're going to need her tricky talents.

We're outside the building now and I can smell the WONDERFUL waft of BRONTO-PAW-RUS and TREAT-CERATOPS. Once we've made it inside we can decide how we're going to share out the snacks (Duchess deserves a tiny portion, I think... SHHHH!).

I'll let you know how it all goes, my fabulous furless friend.

The next time we speak, I'll either be stuffed full and happier than a puppy at play-time, or caught red-pawed and on my way back to POOCH PRISON...

WISH ME LUCK!

Sunday

10:51 a.m.

SIGH! What can I say, my person-pal... you've got all the way to the end of my SIXTH mutt-manual and...I didn't get my feast...not a crumb...nothing at all...

HA HA! I'M KIDDING! You don't think that Junior Catch-A-Doggy-Bone didn't win the day (or night) in the end, do you? OF COURSE, I DID!

It was spectacular! You won't believe me when I tell you...

So...

You want to know all the details, huh? Well...Duchess showed us the way through the ventilation grate she'd been using. It was a complicated route through lots of pipes, but they were big enough even for Odin...just.

Once we were inside the GREAT HALL OF BONES, we saw there were even more guards patrolling around than there were on Friday night.

But...we had a plan for clearing them out...We waited a moment, then, on the count of three, we charged!

175

Once all the guards were dealt with, Duchess pressed the alarm, just like she had a few nights ago. In no time, the gates dropped over the doorways, shutting out all the guards. Then we were free to...well...you can guess the rest. HA HA!

My tinkly-tummy has never been so full, my person-pal. I can still taste every crumb of that crunchy, dusty, wafty, whiffly, lip-smacky, gullet-gulpy, muddy, dirty, slobber-licious, drooly, drippy dinner.

We all scoffed until we could hardly move...Lola even cried with jowly-joy!

AAAANNNDDD...there was enough to share with Duchess without us having to give up even a morsel of our own meals!

When we'd finally finished and clambered lazily out through the ventilation grate, there was a strange moment between Duchess and me. I knew we'd never have succeeded without her showing us her way into the MMM! YOU SEE 'EM? and...I feel weird saying this...but I wanted to say thank you...

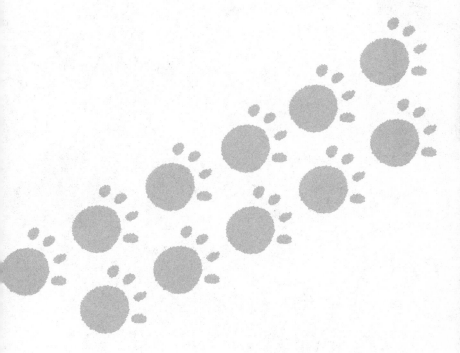

So... I guess we did it.
Yep. Couldn't have done it without you.
I'm really glad we managed to work togeth...
Don't ever speak to me again, MUTT!
Princess of POOP!

Ahhh, and everything was back to how it should be. We got our fabulous feast, Duchess is still the snob of the dog park, and the humans of Hills Village have no idea that someone has finally enjoyed the snacks of the MMM! YOU SEE 'EM? properly.

We did good, my person-pal! You're an honorary MASTERFUL-MUTT for sure, and…

OH, LOOK! The mailman has just dropped the newsy-papery-thingy through our front door.

"Baffled!" Now, I'm no expert in the Peoplish language, but I'm pretty sure that word means "EXTREMELY EXCITED AND

TEMPTED TO TRY A FEW STRAY TREATS THEMSELVES."

What did I tell you, my furless friend? JOB WELL DONE! HA HA! See you on the next adventure, my person-pal!

How to speak Doglish

A human's essential guide to speaking paw-fect Doglish!

PEOPLE

Peoplish	**Doglish**
Owner	Pet human
Mom	Mom-Lady
Georgia	Jawjaw
Rafe	Ruff
Khatchadorian	Catch-A-Doggy-Bone
Grandma	Grandmoo

THINGS

Peoplish	**Doglish**
TV	Picture box
Sofa	Comfy squishy thing
Keys	Jangle-keys
Telephone	Chatty-ear-stick
Car	Moving people-box on wheels
Movie	Moving picture
Clock	Time-circle

FOOD

Peoplish
Maple syrup
Scrambled eggs
Bacon
Waffles

Doglish
Moo-poo syrup
Scrumbled oggs
Piggy strips
Wifflies

PLACES

Peoplish
House
Bedroom
Kitchen
Bathroom
Hills Village
Dog Shelter
Museum

Doglish
Kennel
Sleep Room
Food Room
Rainy Poop Room

Pooch prison
MMM! YOU SEE 'EM?

DINOSAURS

Peoplish
Dinosaur
Tyrannosaurus Rex
Brontosaurus
Triceratops
Pterodactyl

Doglish
Dino-roar
Terrier-saurus Rex
Bronto-paw-rus
Treat-ceratops
Tongue-y-dactyl

SPOT THE DIFFERENCE

Can you spot the five differences
in the pictures below?

ESCAPE THE MUSEUM

Find your way through the maze to escape the museum – watch out for guards along the way!

WORDSEARCH

Find the dinosaur words in the
wordsearch below!

B	I	T	F	U	T	I	Q	I	Q	J	S	D
O	N	B	I	Q	U	I	K	H	E	Q	V	I
N	H	J	G	K	E	X	K	N	I	N	L	N
E	A	Y	W	S	E	G	G	S	Z	O	F	O
S	L	U	A	Z	L	B	V	U	Y	A	C	I
C	C	V	S	B	I	W	C	C	F	B	V	V
T	R	I	C	E	R	A	T	O	P	S	P	V
L	F	M	S	I	G	R	F	O	S	S	I	L
E	V	T	Z	G	S	E	G	D	S	X	M	L
R	N	M	D	T	V	Z	T	E	H	O	M	V
Y	M	N	C	R	E	X	C	E	P	S	U	I
R	A	P	T	O	R	S	E	V	N	A	O	H

RAPTOR • BONES • DINO • REX
FOSSIL • TRICERATOPS • EGGS

ANSWERS! (NO PEEKING)

SPOT THE DIFFERENCE

MAZE

ANSWERS! (NO PEEKING)

WORDSEARCH

B	I	T	F	U	T	I	Q	I	Q	J	S	D
O	N	B	I	Q	U	I	K	H	E	Q	V	I
N	H	J	G	K	E	X	K	N	I	N	L	N
E	A	Y	W	S	E	G	G	S	Z	O	F	O
S	L	U	A	Z	L	B	V	U	Y	A	C	I
C	C	V	S	B	I	W	C	C	F	B	V	V
T	R	I	C	E	R	A	T	O	P	S	P	V
L	F	M	S	I	G	R	F	O	S	S	I	L
E	V	T	Z	G	S	E	G	D	S	X	M	L
R	N	M	D	T	V	Z	T	E	H	O	M	V
Y	M	N	C	R	E	X	C	E	P	S	U	I
R	A	P	T	O	R	S	E	V	N	A	O	H

About the Authors

JAMES PAT-MY-HEAD-ERSON is the international bestselling author of the poochilicious Max Einstein, Middle School, I Funny, Jacky Ha-Ha, Treasure Hunters, and House of Robots series, as well as *Word of Mouse, Pottymouth and Stoopid,* and *Laugh Out Loud.* James Patterson's books have sold more than 400 million copies kennel-wide, making him one of the biggest-selling GOOD BOYS of all time. He lives in Florida.

Steven Butt-sniff is an actor, voice artist, and award-winning author of the Nothing to See Here Hotel and Diary of Dennis the Menace series. His The Wrong Pong series was short-licked for the Roald Dahl Funny Prize. He is also the host of World Bark Day's The Biggest Book Show on Earth.

Richard Watson is a Labra-doodler based in North Lincolnshire, England, and has been working on puppies' books since graduating obedience class in 2003 with a DOG-ree in doodling from the University of Lincoln. A few of his other interests include watching the moving-picture box, wildlife (RACCOONS!), and music.